ANNIE OAKLEY
THE WOMAN WHO NEVER MISSED A SHOT

Retold by
KATHERINE ROSE

Illustrated by
RICHARD MADISON

Cavendish Square
New York

Annie Oakley was born as Phoebe Ann Moses on August 13, 1860, on a small farm near Greenville, Ohio. Her parents were Susan and Jacob Moses, and she had four sisters and a brother. They lived in a rough cabin that had been built by her father. Her parents were poor, and could not afford to educate their children.

As a child, Annie was a tomboy. Her favorite days were when her father would take her hunting with him. Annie was his favorite daughter. She was lively, energetic, talkative, and had more pluck than all her sisters put together.

One cold winter evening, the family had ran of food. Jacob left for the mill on horseback to purchase grain. "Come back soon, Father," said little Annie, who was barely five years old.

"Wait right by the door," he said. "Count slowly to twenty. I'll be back by then," he said with a smile.

Annie counted to twenty, but her father did not come back. He was caught in a severe blizzard. The whole family sat huddled together, praying for his return. Around midnight, they heard a horse's hooves. Annie ran to open the door. Jacob was sitting on the horse, frozen in place.

The entire family rushed to help Jacob inside. But unfortunately, he lost his legs that night due to frostbite. He passed away after that long, cold winter.

Annie's mother now had to support the entire family of six all alone. The children tried to help. They cooked, swept, swabbed, sewed, gathered berries, farmed, and looked after the animals.

But it wasn't enough. The family had to leave their home and move to a smaller farm. Annie wanted to do something to help. "If only Papa were still here to hunt, there would be more food to eat," she thought. Just then, she had an idea. Her father had taught her how to make traps for small birds and animals using cornstalks.

Annie decided to go back into the woods that she loved and catch game for her family. At the age of five, she had picked up her father's skill of making traps to catch birds and other small animals. Once she captured them, she would tie them up and take them home to be cooked.

But the young, ferocious girl was not satisfied. "I'm sure I could bring home much bigger game if only I could use Papa's rifle," she thought.

9

When Annie was eight, she climbed up on a stool, picked up the rifle, and snuck into the woods. She was a born markswoman. She managed to kill a rabbit on her first shot! She was very excited. "Yay! Tonight we can feast on this rabbit!" she thought.

Annie's mother was far from happy. "A woman should know how to cook, clean, and stitch—not how to ride horses and shoot animals! Don't you dare use that rifle again," she said.

But Annie was confident about her hunting ability. She often snuck off to the woods to practice shooting. Slowly, she began to hunt bigger animals, such as deer.

Unfortunately, conditions at home continued to worsen. Susan was forced to send her children to work on other farms. Annie was sent to an infirmary where she was taught how to cook and stitch.

One day a man visited the infirmary. He asked for a young girl who would be able to help him and his wife take care of their newborn baby. "We have a large, sprawling farm. We will even send the girl to school," he said.

"Please, may I go?" Annie asked the head of the infirmary. She nodded her head. She knew that Annie could never be happy indoors doing housework.

Annie went, excited to start her new life. But the couple went back on their word! They made Annie work around the clock.

13

Annie had to wake up
at four o'clock every morning to
milk the cows, tend to the animals,
make breakfast, work on the farm, and
look after the baby. The couple did not
give her enough food to eat, did not send her
to school, and did not even give her medicine
when she became ill. They even hit her, which
left scars on her back and shoulders for the rest
of her life.

Annie decided to go back to her home.
One night, after the family had fallen asleep, she
quietly unlocked the door, crept out, and ran all the
way to the train station.

A kind gentleman took pity on Annie's small, scared face and frail body and paid for her ticket. "Thank you for all your help, sir," she said, taking her seat. "Thank you for saving me from them."

16

Annie's mother welcomed her back with open arms. She had remarried, and had another daughter. Once back home, Annie began to hunt again. She not only fed herself and her family but also sold much of the meat.

People preferred to buy the meat that Annie hunted. She would deliver the meat in such a way that it was easier to clean and tasted better.

Annie started getting orders from hotels. She earned more money than her mother and stepfather and was able to save enough to pay the family's mortgage. She did this when she was just fifteen years old!

One day, one of Annie's customers, a hotel owner, invited her to participate in a shooting contest that was to be held in his hotel. The renowned marksman, Frank Butler, was also going to participate.

"A fifteen-year-old girl?" asked Frank with a laugh when he heard who his competition was going to be. The challenge was to hit twenty-five targets. Frank managed to hit twenty-four out of the twenty-five. Annie looked straight ahead at the targets, took careful aim, and BAM! BAM! BAM! She hit all twenty-five.

Frank was so smitten by Annie's skill that he proposed. The two married the next year. She was very happy with her new life and loved her husband deeply. She continued shooting as a hobby.

Six years after they married, Annie performed in one of Frank's shows for the first time. His assistant had fallen ill, and Annie filled in for her. It was at this time that Annie took on the stage name of Oakley.

They toured the country for a few years, performing at many shows and exhibitions along with their dog. At one such show in Minnesota, Sitting Bull, a well-known Native American spiritual leader, saw Annie perform. He was reminded of his own daughter. The two soon became good friends. He even adopted her and named her "Little Sure Shot."

Annie's career took off, and there was no turning back. Annie and Frank were then asked to tour along with Buffalo Bill's Wild West Show. This was one of the most famous performances of the time and highlighted Buffalo Bill's adventures in the West.

Annie was the star of Buffalo Bill's show. Soon, Frank stopped performing and became her manager and agent.

For the next eight years, Annie toured the world and had many adventures. She performed for the Queen of England, won many medals and trophies, and was invited to many big events. Everywhere she went, the newspapers wrote about her and her prowess.

So great was Annie's skill that she could shoot holes in the center of playing cards that were tossed in the air. Another one of her famous tricks was to shoot through the center of a coin that had been tossed in the air before it touched the ground.

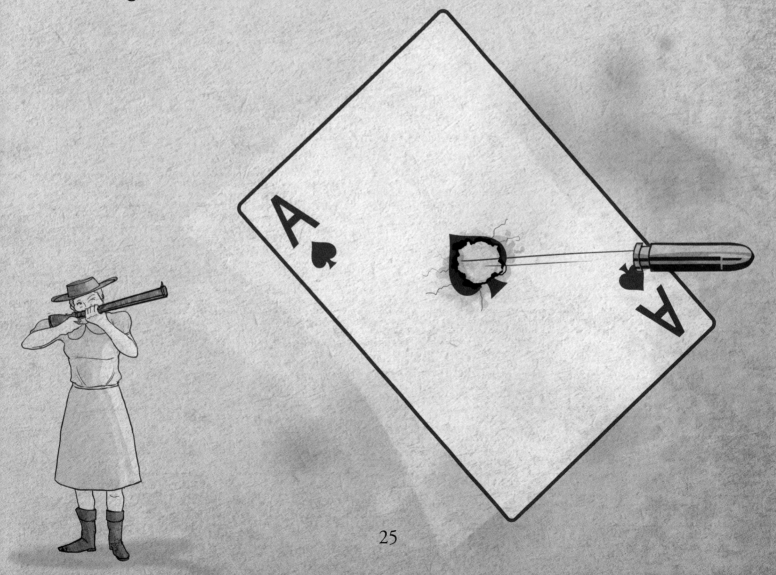

Annie never forgot her roots. She remembered how it felt to sleep on a hungry stomach, and how she yearned to study. She gave much of her money to the poor, and performed many other acts of charity. "If I spend one dollar foolishly, I see the tear-stained faces of little children who are beaten as I was," she said whenever anyone asked her why she gave so much away.

She also said that women should be taught how to use firearms as a form of self-defense. She took part in the women's suffrage movement and fought for equal rights for women.

During World War I, Annie even offered to train a regimen of women volunteers to fight in the war, but her offer was rejected.

At the age of fifty-three, Frank and Annie retired from traveling shows, but continued to perform. She even set a new record at the age of sixty-two! This was a year and a half after a car accident that nearly killed her.

Unfortunately, Annie's recovery did not last long. She fell ill and passed away in 1926.

ABOUT ANNIE OAKLEY

Annie was a woman who made her mark in a man's world during an era that made it incredibly difficult to do so. Apart from having views on gender equality that were progressive for her time, she was also well-known for her modesty and philanthropy.

Although she has been portrayed as the true "Western cowgirl," she did not actually hail from the West, but was born and raised in Ohio. She gained this reputation only because of her participation in Western shows.

WORDS TO KNOW

Frostbite: When a person is exposed to extreme cold, and a part of the body, such as fingers and toes, freezes or almost freezes, the condition is called frostbite.

Infirmary: A hospital-like establishment in which the sick and the elderly receive care.

Prowess: Superior skill in a particular field.

Smitten: Fallen head over heels in love.

Stage name: The name under which a person performs on stage; not necessarily the person's actual name.

Women's suffrage: Earlier in U.S. history, women did not have the right to vote or run for a political office. In a fight for these rights, America's women's suffrage movement began in the late 1800s and gained support and momentum through the early 1900s.

TO FIND OUT MORE

BOOKS:

Krensky, Stephen. *Shooting for the Moon.* New York: Farrar, Straus and Giroux (2001).

Macy, Sue. *Bull's-Eye: A Photobiography of Annie Oakley.* Washington, DC: National Geographic Children's Books (2006).

Spinner, Stephanie. *Who was Annie Oakley?* New York: Grosset & Dunlap (2001).

WEBSITES:

http://www.pbs.org/wgbh/americanexperience/films/oakley/
Watch a documentary on Annie's life on this site.

http://www.britannica.com/EBchecked/topic/423468/Annie-Oakley
This site gives you factual information on the life of Annie Oakley.

http://www.annieoakleyfoundation.org/life.html
This site is maintained by Annie's grand nieces and nephews. They write about her from memory and family stories.

Published in 2014 by Cavendish Square Publishing, LLC
303 Park Avenue South, Suite 1247, New York, NY 10010
Copyright © 2014 by Cavendish Square Publishing, LLC
First Edition

This publication represents the opinions and views of the author based on his or her personal experience, knowledge, and research. The information in this book serves as a general guide only. The author and publisher have used their best efforts in preparing this book and disclaim liability rising directly or indirectly from the use and application of this book.

CPSIA Compliance Information: Batch #WW14CSQ
All websites were available and accurate when this book was sent to press.
LIBRARY OF CONGRESS CATALOGING-IN-PUBLICATION DATA
Rose, Katherine.
Annie Oakley/Katherine Rose.
pages cm. — (American legends and folktales)
ISBN 978-1-62712-286-3 (hardcover) ISBN 978-1-62712-287-0 (paperback) ISBN 978-1-62712-288-7 (ebook)
1. Oakley, Annie, 1860-1926. 2. Shooters of firearms—United States—Biography—Juvenile literature.
3. Women entertainers—United States—Biography—Juvenile literature.
I. Title.
GV1157.O3R67 2014
799.3092—dc23

Printed in the United States of America

Editorial Director: Dean Miller
Art Director: Jeffrey Talbot

Content and Design by quadrum
www.quadrumltd.com